Pe/cn

return

D1080722

Princess Katie's Kittens

Princess Katie's Kittens

Collect all the kittens!

Pixie at the Palace
Bella at the Ball
Poppy and the Prince

Coming Soon:

Suki in the Snow
Tilly and the Tiara
Pebbles and the Puppy

PrincessKatiesKittens.co.uk

Princess Katie's Kittens

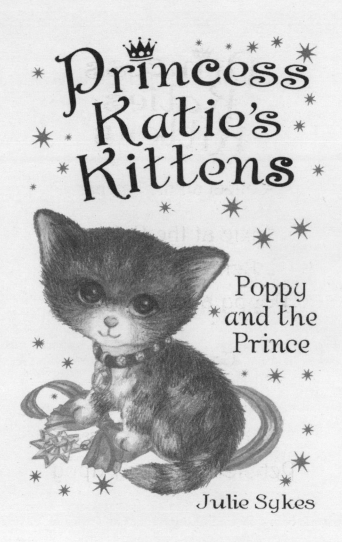

Poppy
and the
Prince

Julie Sykes

PICCADILLY PRESS • LONDON

For
Harald and Natascha Vangerow

First published in Great Britain in 2012
by Piccadilly Press Ltd,
5 Castle Road, London NW1 8PR
www.piccadillypress.co.uk

Text copyright © Julie Sykes, 2012

All rights reserved. No part of this publication
may be reproduced, stored in a retrieval system,
or transmitted in any form or by any means electronic,
mechanical, photocopying, recording or otherwise, without
the prior permission of the copyright owner.

The right of Julie Sykes to be identified as Author of this
work has been asserted by her in accordance with the
Copyright, Designs and Patents Act, 1988

A catalogue record for this book is available
from the British Library

ISBN: 978 1 84812 241 3 (paperback)

1 3 5 7 9 10 8 6 4 2

Printed and bound by CPI Group (UK) Ltd, Croydon, CR0 4YY
Cover design by Simon Davis
Cover illustration by Sue Hellard

Chapter 1

Cousin Eddie

Princess Katie and her best friend Becky Philips were on their way to the stables. It was the perfect day for a ride. The spring sun was warm and there wasn't a cloud in the soft blue sky. Red squirrels chattered from the trees and a peacock was parading on the lawn, his amazing tail spread out like a green-and-blue

fan. They passed the rose garden, where the queen was talking with the head gardener.

'Hello, girls,' she called. 'I've just chosen some orange roses for Edward's room but I can't decide between the red or cream ones for your Uncle Paul and Auntie Meg. What do you think?'

Edward, or Eddie as he was nicknamed,

was Katie's nine-year-old cousin. He lived in the west of Tula so they didn't see each other very often, but when he and his parents — Katie's aunt and uncle — visited they stayed for several days.

'Why not have red *and* cream,' said Katie. 'They'll look great together.'

The queen smiled. 'Thanks, that's a great idea.'

'I can't wait to see Eddie again,' said Katie, walking on. 'Do you remember the camp we built when he was here last year?'

'On the island!' exclaimed Becky. 'It was such fun. My favourite bit was when your uncle Paul fell out of the rowing boat coming ashore.'

'That was funny!' Katie chuckled. 'This time I thought we could have a picnic in the maze. And we'll go riding, and play with the kittens.'

'Does Eddie like cats?' asked Becky.

'Everyone likes kittens,' said Katie, smiling confidently.

The following day, as Katie arrived home from school, a large blue car passed hers on the drive.

'Your aunt and uncle are here,' remarked Mr Bentley, the driver, as the blue car pulled off towards the royal garages.

The moment Katie's silver Rolls-Royce stopped, she jumped out.

'Thank you, Mr Bentley,' she called, remembering her manners as she raced up the palace steps.

The hall was full of suitcases and the butler was organising staff to carry them to the east tower. Hopping round the luggage, Katie went along to the drawing room where her parents received guests. She pushed open the door and there were the Duke and Duchess of Fairsky, otherwise known as Aunty Meg and Uncle Paul!

Katie dropped them a curtsy.

'Princess Katie,' squealed Auntie Meg, 'my favourite niece! Come here and give me a hug.'

Katie was about to run to her aunt when she stopped in surprise. Who was that tall, gangly boy standing awkwardly by the fireplace?

'Eddie,' she said, uncertainly. 'But you're miles taller than me now!'

'It's Edward or Ed,' he said. 'Eddie's a bit babyish.'

Katie blushed, but no one noticed as Auntie Meg

smothered her with an enormous hug. 'Oh my goodness, you've grown too,' she said, 'and look how long your hair is!'

There was a knock on the door and a maid entered, carrying a tray with a china teapot, milk and cups.

'You and Edward don't have to stay for tea,' said the queen kindly. 'I'm sure you'd much rather go and play.'

Katie smiled politely to cover up her sudden shyness. Even though they were the same age, Edward seemed much older now. Whatever would they do together?

Then she had a brainwave.

'Would you like to come and see my kittens?' she asked.

Edward hesitated. 'All right.'

'There are six,' said Katie as she led the

way to the boot room. 'Becky and I rescued them when someone left them in the woods. You remember Becky, don't you?'

'No,' said Edward.

'She's the girl we built the camp with last time you came.'

Edward shrugged. 'I don't remember.'

It wasn't a good start. But maybe Edward would be friendlier once he'd met the kittens. When he saw how cute they were, it would be impossible for him to stay grumpy.

To Katie's dismay, Edward wasn't the

least bit interested in her cats. He hung back and didn't try to stroke them, even when Poppy the tortoiseshell kitten climbed on his foot and butted her head against his leg.

Edward might be feeling
shy too, Katie thought. If she
left him on his own, maybe
he'd find it easier to make
friends with the kittens.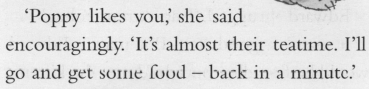

'Poppy likes you,' she said
encouragingly. 'It's almost their teatime. I'll
go and get some food – back in a minute.'

Edward opened his mouth to say something
but Katie pretended not to see. She was sure
that by the time she came back with food,
Edward and Poppy would be great friends.

Poppy was pleased to see Katie. She loved the
cuddles she got when the princess came to
visit and today she'd brought someone new

with her. Poppy said hello to Katie and, when the boy ignored her, she went and sat on his foot.

Then Katie left the room. Edward stood very still. Poppy rubbed her head on his leg and immediately she felt him tense. That was strange. Poppy nudged him again, showing that she only wanted to make friends.

Edward shook his foot. Poppy hung on in surprise, her claws gripping onto the shoe's laces.

'Get off,' said Edward, kicking his foot harder.

At once, Poppy lost her grip and slid to the floor.

'Meow!' she said indignantly.

Edward gave a low chuckle.

Thoughtfully, Poppy fixed him with her big green eyes. *I get it! It's a game.*

Eagerly she climbed back onto Edward's shoe.

'Get off!' growled Edward, kicking his foot harder this time.

With a startled yowl, Poppy slid to the floor, landing on her back. Quickly, she righted herself and, fluffing out her fur, glared at Edward. If he was going to be that rough then she didn't want to play any more. Edward laughed and Poppy stalked away crossly.

'Wait,' called Edward, coming after her.

Poppy hesitated. He sounded friendly. Perhaps she'd give him another chance.

'Good cat,' said Edward encouragingly. 'Come to Ed.'

He squatted down and rubbed his fingers against his thumb in an interesting way. Poppy couldn't help herself. She knew that sign – Katie did it when she wanted her to come for a cuddle. Eagerly, she trotted back to Edward, putting her paw on his knee as he bent down beside her. Once again he tensed, then, taking a deep breath, he lifted her up carefully, holding her out in front of him.

A cuddle!

Thinking Edward was going to give her a cuddle, Poppy purred with delight. She started to relax but Edward put her back on his foot and, before she knew what was happening, he'd kicked her off again.

Poppy landed with a bump at the moment the door opened.

Chapter 2

The Picnic Hamper

'What's going on?'

Katie rushed into the room and scooped Poppy into her arms. The little kitten's heart was racing with fright. Katie glared at Edward waiting for an answer.

'We were playing,' said Edward with a smile. 'He was enjoying it.'

'He? *Her* name's Poppy. She wasn't enjoying it. She's trembling.'

Edward pulled a face. 'She kept climbing back onto my foot. She'd have run away if she didn't want to play.' Katie stroked the top of Poppy's silky brown head.

The kitten seemed much calmer now and nuzzled her nose in Katie's hand. Maybe she was being a little hard on Edward. He didn't have any pets so perhaps he didn't know how to treat them. Deciding to give him the benefit of the doubt, Katie said kindly, 'Kittens are like babies. You have to be gentle or you can hurt them.'

'Really!' said Edward, nodding seriously. 'So no biting or scratching, then?'

Katie frowned. Was Edward teasing her?

'No,' she said uncertainly.

'Good,' said Edward. 'No biting or scratching. I'll remember that. And so must you, Popsie. Can I go to my room now? I hope it's got a television because I brought my new Playstation with me.'

'It's *Poppy*,' said
Katie, putting the
kitten back in her
basket. 'There is a
television, but you
won't have much time
for Playstation. Becky
and I have planned lots

of things to do while you're here. We're
having a picnic in the maze tomorrow, riding
the next day and —'

'Oh goodie,' said Edward, cutting her off.
'I can hardly wait. *Not!* I'll stick with my
Playstation, thanks. Mazes are for babies.'

'No, they are not,' said Katie indignantly.
'Mazes are for everyone. Becky and I still get
lost in ours. It's great fun. And you should
see the picnics that Becky's mum makes.

She's our housekeeper and her picnics are famous.'

Edward shrugged. 'I prefer banquets. That's what our palace is famous for. The last one we had went on all night. We had fifty tables covered with food. There were six bands and we danced until sunrise, and then breakfast was served. I was so hungry I had three eggs with mine.'

Katie smiled politely. She was very surprised that Aunty Meg

had let Edward stay up all night. Unless he was exaggerating!

'Sorry, but there are no banquets planned for this week. I think Grandma and Grandad are visiting on one of the days. And the Prime Minister is coming for dinner. Your room is in the east tower. Follow me and I'll show you where.'

Later that evening, everyone gathered in the family lounge for a mug of hot chocolate before bed.

'I hear you're having a picnic in the maze tomorrow,' said Aunty Meg. 'It sounds great fun. I'm tempted to come along too.'

'Picnics are boring,' said Edward.

Aunty Meg frowned. 'Edward! That's rude.'

'The picnics at Starlight Towers are *never* boring,' said Uncle Paul. 'You'll have great fun.'

A slow smile curled on Edward's lips. 'I was only joking. It will be fun. I can carry the picnic hamper if you like. I'll go and get

it from the kitchens tomorrow morning. I'll meet you at the maze, Katie.'

Katie stared at Edward over the top of her mug of hot chocolate. There was a secretive expression on his face that made her feel uneasy. He looked like he was planning something. But Edward kept smiling. Maybe she was being unfair? Pushing her doubts away, Katie smiled back.

'Thanks. I'll come with you if you like. The picnic hamper is going to be heavy.'

'I'll manage,' said Edward firmly. 'I'll meet you at the maze.'

Early the following morning, Katie and Becky met to feed the kittens and play with them before they went out.

'They're getting bigger every day!' exclaimed Becky, lifting Poppy out of the basket to give her a cuddle.

'And livelier,' said Katie, watching Bella and Suki play-fighting and tumbling over each other.

It was good fun rolling balls for the kittens to chase and teasing them with the jingly mouse. The kittens ran around like crazy

until, one by one, they started to tire. Poppy pawed at Katie's leg, asking for a cuddle. Katie picked her up. Poppy purred ecstatically, snuggling into her arms. She was most indignant when she was put back in her basket.

'Sorry, Poppy, but we've got to go now,' Katie said. 'We'll come and see you later.'

Katie and Becky ran through the gardens so they wouldn't be late to meet Edward. They reached the maze before him and, panting loudly, collapsed on the bench outside.

'We needn't have run after all,' said Becky five minutes later, when Edward still hadn't arrived.

'I hope he's coming,' said Katie. Uneasily, she remembered Edward's secretive smile when he'd offered to collect the picnic hamper.

Ten minutes later, Katie stood up. 'I'd better go and see what's keeping him,' she said.

'There he is!' said Becky. 'He's just passing the rose garden.'

Edward was carrying an enormous picnic

hamper. He was red in the face and walking slowly.

'Well done,' said Katie, running to meet him with Becky. 'Here, it's our turn now. We normally carry it together.'

'If you want,' said Edward, dumping the hamper on the ground.

'What was that?' said Katie in surprise. 'It sounded like the hamper squeaked.'

'That was me,' said Edward, not meeting her eye. 'My stomach rumbled. Hurry up, or is the hamper too heavy for you?'

'Definitely not,' said Katie, as she and Becky both took the handle.

Now Edward wasn't carrying the hamper, he seemed to be in a hurry. He practically ran to the maze and disappeared inside.

'Wait!' called Katie. 'It's easy to get lost.'

'Huh!' sneered Edward. 'I never get lost in the maze at home.'

Becky raised her eyebrows and Katie grinned back at her.

'Good,' Katie called, trying hard to sound friendly. 'Wait for us, then, because we *always* get lost!'

Entering the maze was like walking through a multicoloured tunnel. Thick green bushes laced with brightly coloured flowers stretched high above Katie's head.

'It's grown since we were last here,' she said, pushing aside an overhanging branch.

'Yeah, it's rubbish,' said Edward. 'It needs cutting.'

'I like it like this,' said Becky loyally. 'It's more mysterious. What's the matter, Katie? Why are you frowning?'

Katie stopped walking. 'It's the hamper. It keeps squeaking. Listen.'

Becky listened, her eyes screwed up with concentration. Edward turned away and Katie noticed his shoulders were shaking as if he was laughing.

'There it is again!' she said.

'I heard it too,' said Becky.

They lowered the hamper to the ground and Katie fumbled with the buckles. She lifted the lid but, as she went to peer inside, something jumped out at her.

'Poppy!' she exclaimed. 'How did you get in there?'

Chapter 3

A Stowaway

Edward could hardly stand up for laughing.

'A stowaway,' he chortled. 'Has she eaten the prawn sandwiches?'

Katie's eyes narrowed suspiciously. 'How do you know she likes prawns?'

'She's a cat,' said Edward, airily. 'They all like fish.'

'But how did she get inside the hamper?' asked Katie. 'We were playing with her in the boot room until we left to meet you. Did you put her in there? You did, didn't you? What if she gets lost in the maze?'

'Keep your tiara on!' said Edward. 'She's a cat. They're good at finding their way home.'

Katie was furious with Edward but, remembering she was the host and it wasn't polite to get angry, she tried her best to stay calm.

'Poppy's only little,' she said. 'She's only just had the injections she needs before she's allowed outside. None of the kittens have been out of the palace since we found them. Poppy could easily get lost. Now I'll have to take her back to the boot room.'

'Why?' asked Edward. 'She likes being out, just look at her.'

Poppy did look very happy. Inquisitively, she looked around.

'Maybe it *is* about time we let the kittens outside,' said Becky. 'Unless you want to keep them as house cats?'

Katie shook her head. Cats loved the out-doors and it wasn't fair to keep hers locked up. Starlight Palace had lots of gardens to play in and there were no roads nearby. But she was cross that Edward had taken Poppy out when it should have been her decision.

'Poppy can stay this time,' she said, 'but everyone has to watch her so she doesn't wander off and get lost. Next time you want to take a kitten anywhere, Edward, please ask me first.'

'Whatever.' Turning his back on Katie, he kicked at a stone. Poppy dashed after it, making Edward laugh.

Katie was cross. That was so typical! Now Edward would think he was better at looking after cats than her.

Becky reached for Katie's hand and squeezed it gently. 'Don't worry,' she said. 'We'll look after her.'

Katie squeezed Becky's hand back. 'Thanks,' she whispered.

Picking up the picnic hamper, Katie and Becky followed Edward until they reached a fork in the path.

'Go right,' called Katie.

At the next fork Edward turned left. Katie wasn't paying much attention. She kept looking back to check that Poppy was still following. The little cat was clearly enjoying herself. Her tail was high, her ears were pricked and her green eyes were bright with curiosity.

'Is it straight ahead here?' asked Becky, as they came to a crossroads.

Katie hesitated. 'I thought it was left.'

'The bushes have grown so tall it all looks different,' said Becky. 'Let's go left, then. It doesn't matter if it's wrong. That's half the fun.'

Edward tutted as if it mattered a lot.

The path led to a dead end. Edward sighed heavily but Katie and Becky giggled as they retraced their footsteps. It took much longer than usual to find the middle, especially because they had to keep waiting for Poppy, but, as the path began to zigzag, they knew they were almost there.

'Here, Poppy!' called Katie.

The kitten had stopped and was reaching up with her front paws, as if she might try to climb the bush.

'What's she after?' asked Becky.

'A bird,' said Katie. 'Can you hear it calling?'

Standing very
still, Becky tilted
her head to listen.
'Yes, and it doesn't
sound happy. This
way, Poppy. Leave
the bird alone. Wait
till you see what's at the middle of the maze.
You're going to love it.'

Reluctantly, Poppy stopped trying to climb
the bush and followed the girls. She didn't
know why they were in such a hurry. There
were lots of things to explore here. The
bushes that towered on either side of her
like enormous green walls were packed with
insects and animals. Their different scents

and noises were driving Poppy mad with excitement.

That bird shouting so angrily was protecting a nest full of tiny chicks. With her sharp ears, Poppy could hear them squawking for food. She was longing to climb up and have a closer look, but Katie and Becky kept calling her. A stripy insect buzzed across her path and landed on a leaf. Poppy's insides fizzed excitedly as she pounced on it.

'Poppy, no!' cried Katie.

The stripy thing flew into the air. Poppy leapt after it but missed again.

'Poppy!' squeaked Katie. 'You'll get stung.'

The kitten stared in surprise, not under-
standing why the princess sounded upset.
Poppy wasn't going to hurt the wasp. She
only wanted to play with it.

Katie crouched down and rubbed her
fingers and thumb together.

Poppy moved closer and was rewarded
with a stroke. She couldn't get enough of
Katie and Becky stroking and cuddling her.
She rubbed her silky body against Katie's
legs, purring happily as Katie scratched her
on the top of the top of the head.

'Come on, slow-paws,' said Katie, moving
on again.

Ignoring the interesting rustles and
squeaks coming from the bushes, Poppy
concentrated on the lovely smell drifting

from the basket as she padded after the girls. The path began to zigzag until it ended unexpectedly in a bush. Poppy stared at it in surprise. Surely this wasn't what the girls were so keen to show her?

Putting the picnic basket down, Princess Katie stepped right up to the bush and plunged her hand into its middle.

Poppy's ears suddenly twitched. *What was that?*

Spinning round, she stuck her nose into the hedge behind her to investigate.

Mouse! There was no mistaking that musky smell. On silent paws, Poppy wriggled after it.

Chapter 4

Eddie Is a Pain

Delving around in the bushes, Kate's fingers finally gripped hold of the doorknob cleverly hidden by leaves. She turned it, then pushed, grinning triumphantly as a section of the bush suddenly swung inwards like a door.

Edward shoved his hands in his pockets, looking bored, but Becky's brown eyes shone.

'I love this bit,' she breathed happily.

'We're here. This is the middle,' said Katie, stepping aside to let Edward go first.

'Is this it?' asked Edward, but Katie hardly heard him.

'Where's Poppy?' she asked.

'She was here a minute ago,' said Becky,

looking around. 'Poppy. Here, kitty! Where are you?'

Katie felt suddenly hot and her heart banged loudly. It had taken just seconds for Poppy to wander off, but it could take hours to find her if she was lost in the maze.

'Poppy!' she called frantically.

When Poppy didn't appear, Katie swiftly walked back along the path.

'Wait!' called Becky, running after her. 'She won't have gone that far.'

'She might have.' Katie kept hurrying along

the zigzag path calling, 'Poppy! Here, puss! Where are you?'

When she couldn't see her, Katie broke into a run.

'Katie, wait! I can hear something.'

'What?' Katie spun round hopefully.

'It came from in there,' whispered Becky, pointing.

Katie stood very still. At first the only thing she could hear was her own heart thundering, but then she heard a soft rustling. She stared at the hedge. The leaves were trembling as if an animal were slowly creeping through it. Squatting down, she stared through the branches.

'Poppy!' she exclaimed, her breath rushing out in relief. 'I see you. You naughty thing! Come here.'

Half crawling under the hedge Katie reached out and grabbed Poppy round the waist.

'Meow!'

Poppy was not pleased at being caught and tried to wriggle free.

'Oh no you don't!' Ignoring the twigs scratching her hands, Katie pulled Poppy backwards. 'Naughty girl. You gave me such a fright.' She held Poppy against her face for a second. Poppy glared back, her green eyes indignant. Katie and Becky burst out laughing.

'Looks like she was after a bird,' chuckled Becky. 'You'll have to get her a collar with a bell on.'

'Good idea,' said Katie. 'Come on, you! Now we've lost Edward.'

'And he's got the picnic,' said Becky.

They ran back and stepped through the secret door that led to the middle of the maze.

'Look, there's Edward. He's already at the top of the fort,' said Katie.

'And there's the picnic,' said Becky pointing to a large rectangular table surrounded with eight chairs and shaded with a sun umbrella.

'Race you to the top!' said Becky.

'I don't know . . .' Katie wasn't keen on

leaving Poppy on her own in case she wandered off again.

'Put Poppy in the play park,' said Becky, guessing her concern. 'The fence is high enough to stop her going anywhere.'

'Good idea.'

Leaving Poppy by the swings, they ran back across the neatly clipped grass and, ducking under the archway, they entered the fort. On one side, a wooden staircase led to the upper levels. Becky reached the stairs first with Katie close behind. By the time they reached the third floor they were both panting heavily.

'Beat you,' said Becky, running across the top to the final staircase that led to the tower.

'Not yet!' said Katie, overtaking and going ahead.

On the last stair Becky drew alongside. They reached the top together and collapsed in a giggling heap.

'Tie!' gasped Katie.

'For you two, but I won,' boasted Edward, leaning against the flagpole in the tower's centre. 'I've been here for ages.'

Exchanging a smile with Becky, Katie resisted the urge to tell Edward that it was his fault they'd been delayed.

'I forgot how big it is,' said Katie, gazing at the maze spread out before her.

'It's not *that* big,' said Edward. 'It's a bit babyish really. I'm starving. Let's have lunch.'

With a last look at the maze, the girls followed Edward back down to the ground.

While Katie let Poppy out of the play park, Becky and Edward set out the picnic. It was one of Mrs Philips's best. There were four different types of sandwich, a pot of fresh prawns, tiny cooked sausages, neat sticks of carrot and cucumber, crisps, little cakes with coloured icing, and cherries fresh from the palace hothouse. Poppy purred ecstatically as Katie and Becky fed

her tiny pieces of sausage and prawns.

'This is brilliant,' said Katie, sipping fizzy peach juice through a pink straw.

'You should have been at our banquet,' said Edward. 'We had king prawns and champagne.'

Katie smothered a giggle as she fed Poppy another prawn. She was sure Uncle Paul hadn't let Edward drink the champagne.

'Poppy will do anything for prawns,' said Edward. 'That's how I got her into the basket.' Picking the largest prawn in the tub, he held it out to Poppy. She went to him at once, daintily sniffing the prawn he was dangling between his fingers. But as she reached up to take it, Edward pulled the prawn back and popped it in his mouth.

'Mmmm, delicious,' he said, noisily smacking his lips.

Poppy pawed at his leg indignantly.

'Aw, sorry, Pops,' said Edward, not sounding in the least bit sorry. 'Here, have this one.'

Reaching for another prawn Edward held it out to her.

Trustingly, Poppy went to take the prawn but Edward snatched it away again. Poppy's ears went back and she swished her tail.

'Edward!' Katie exclaimed. 'That wasn't very nice.'

'But it was *so* funny,' chuckled Edward, his mouth full of prawn. 'Here, Poppy, you can have this one,' he said as Poppy nosed the prawn.

'Stop it,' said Katie.

'Ouch!' Edward dropped the prawn he was teasing Poppy with and held out his finger. 'She scratched me.'

'It was your fault,' said Katie. 'You shouldn't tease animals. They don't understand.'

'It's only a little scratch,' said Becky. 'It  hasn't even drawn blood.' Edward stood up. 'I'll get you for that,' he said, pointing at Poppy.

'You mustn't! It wasn't her fault,' said Katie anxiously.

Edward ignored her. 'I'm going back to the palace,' he said.

Katie was cross with Edward and concerned that he might do something silly to Poppy, but it was still her responsibility to look after him.

'We haven't had any cake yet,' she said. 'Let's finish the picnic and then we'll all go back.'

'No,' said Edward as he started for the exit.

'Wait,' called Katie. 'I'm coming with you.'

'Don't bother. I won't get lost,' said Edward scornfully, but he hovered by the hidden door as Katie and Becky hurriedly packed up the picnic things.

No one said much as they made their way out of the maze with the picnic hamper. Katie barely took her eyes off Poppy, just in case she ran off again. At last, they were back in the palace gardens and Edward went indoors without waiting for the girls.

'What a waste of a picnic,' sighed Katie.

'It doesn't have to be. Let's finish it here,' said Becky, pointing at the newly mown lawn.

'It would be a shame to miss the cake,' said Katie, grinning.

They laid the food out on the picnic rug and sat down to enjoy it. Poppy was tired after her busy morning. Climbing onto Katie's lap, she settled down with her eyes closed. Katie was starting her second cupcake when the queen came along.

'Where's Edward?' she asked in surprise.

'He didn't want to stay in the maze or finish the picnic,' said Katie.

'Katie! Edward's your guest. Put that kitten back in the boot room and go and ask Edward what he would like to do,' said the queen crossly.

Katie wanted to explain how awful Edward had been, but, remembering princesses didn't tell tales, unless someone was about to do something dangerous, she stopped herself and said, 'Sorry. I'll go and find him now.'

'How long is Edward staying? Becky asked, as they took Poppy back to the boot room.

'A whole week,' groaned Katie. 'Whatever will we do with him?'

'We'll think of something.'

Katie nodded. But finding ways of entertaining Edward wasn't the real problem. A bigger worry was his threat to get Poppy back. What if he did something silly and accidentally hurt her?

Chapter 5

Out for a Ride

At breakfast the next day, Katie suggested that she, Becky and Edward go for a ride. Edward liked that idea.

'I miss Arrow. I ride him every day.'

'Is he your new pony?' asked Katie. 'Have you still got Patches?'

'Arrow's a horse,' said Edward. 'I'm far too

big to ride ponies now. We gave Patches to the groom's daughter.'

Katie nodded. Edward had grown a lot since she'd last seen him. After breakfast, she ran upstairs and changed into her favourite lilac jodhpurs, then she went to the boot room to get her riding boots. The door was ajar. Katie hurried inside and found Edward

leaning over the kittens'
basket. A shiver of fear
went through her.
'What are you doing?'
she asked.

Sliding something into
his pocket, Edward spun round.

'Just making friends with Poppy,' he said.

Was she imagining things or did Edward
look guilty? He wouldn't look at her and he
kept his hand over his pocket as if he had
something he didn't want her to see.

Suddenly, Edward
reached out and
gently stroked Poppy.
At first, the kitten
stayed stiff and her
green eyes were

wary, but after a while her body relaxed and she started purring. When Edward pulled his hand away, Poppy nudged it and mewed for more.

'She likes me,' said Edward, sounding a little smug.

'Yes!' Katie smiled, deciding she'd let her imagination get the better of her.

Walking to the stables, Edward was more like the cousin Katie remembered and liked. They talked about horses and how Edward was hoping to compete with Arrow. When they reached the yard, Becky was already mounted on a chestnut pony and holding Misty.

'Thanks,' said Katie, taking the reins and

checking the girth that held the saddle on was done up tightly before she mounted.

Miss Blaze, the riding teacher, led a cute palomino pony into the yard.

'Hello, you must be Edward. You're riding Honey today.'

Edward scowled. 'I'm not riding *that*. She's far too little.'

'She's a good size and she's very strong,' said Miss Blaze, pleasantly. 'Do you have a hat? If not there are spare ones in the tack room over there.'

'I never wear a hat. Not unless I'm competing,' said Edward.

'And I never let anyone ride without one,' said Miss Blaze, firmly.

Edward stared at her for a moment, then with a cross sigh he marched into the tack room and came back with a hat.

'This pony's far too small for me,' he grumbled.

'Your stirrups are just too short,' said Princess Katie, letting them down for him, and giving the girth a quick check. 'There, that's better.'

Katie loved riding more than anything

else, but it wasn't much fun with Edward around. He moaned constantly. Honey was too small, the ride was too slow. He wanted to do some jumping. After a while he kept hanging back and then cantering to catch up. It unsettled Misty to have another horse coming up fast behind her and she laid back her ears and pranced nervously instead of walking nicely.

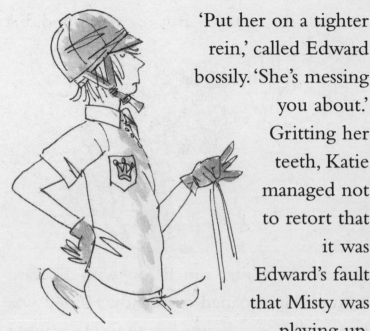

'Put her on a tighter rein,' called Edward bossily. 'She's messing you about.' Gritting her teeth, Katie managed not to retort that it was Edward's fault that Misty was playing up.

Edward spent the rest of the ride grumbling about how slow Honey was and how much faster Arrow could go. They cantered down a path where there was a series of fallen logs to jump. Katie loved the feeling of flying though the air as she and Misty cleared the jumps. But even that didn't please Edward.

'Too easy,' he said in a bored voice. 'I jump much higher at home.'

When they got back in the yard, Katie and

Becky dismounted and took the saddles and bridles off their ponies. Edward sat on Honey, letting his reins hang loose.

'Are you all right, Edward?' asked Katie.

'I'm waiting for someone to take my horse,' he answered.

'It's do-it-yourself here,' said Katie cheerfully. 'Miss Blaze says it's important that we

learn to look after a horse as well as how to ride one.'

Edward looked astonished. 'I'm not doing that,' he said.

Before Katie could answer, Miss Blaze came out of the feed room carrying a bucket of pony nuts. Honey threw up her head, whinnied with excitement and trotted towards her.

'Eek!' squeaked Edward.

He snatched for the reins but couldn't reach them as they were dangling against Honey's side. As Honey swerved to avoid a bale of hay Edward lost his balance. He slid sideways and fell off, landing on the hay bale and splitting it open.

Chapter 6

Poppy Gets Wet

Edward looked so funny lying on his back, with his legs in the air and straw sticking out of his hair, that Katie burst out laughing. Becky giggled too, clutching her stomach with one hand and holding on to her pony with the other.

'Here, take Misty for me,' Katie chuckled,

passing her reins to Becky.

She held out a hand to pull Edward up. 'Are you all right? Lucky you had a soft landing.'

Edward screwed up his face in anger. He refused Katie's help as he scrambled to his feet.

'Stupid place to leave a bale of hay,' he said crossly. 'Our grooms aren't allowed to leave anything in the yard. It's untidy.'

Katie bit back a sigh. She was getting tired of hearing how much better everything was at Edward's palace.

'Where are you going?' she asked, as Edward stormed out of the yard.

'Back to my room.'

'Wait,' said Katie. 'Let me turn the ponies out in the field and then I'll come with you.'

'I know where I'm going.' Edward walked faster.

Becky rolled her eyes. 'I'm glad he's your cousin, not mine,' she muttered.

Miss Blaze caught hold of Honey, who was trying to get her nose in the bucket of pony nuts.

'I'll put her out in the field,' said Katie.

'Are you sure, Princess? I can turn all the ponies out if you want to go after Prince Edward.'

'I'm sure,' said Katie, thinking it would be a good idea to give Edward time to calm down before she followed him.

Katie and Becky gave the ponies a quick groom with a dandy brush then turned them out in the big field behind the stables, before they slowly walked back to the palace together.

'I'd better go and find Edward,' sighed Katie as they went indoors.

'Good luck,' said Becky cheerfully.

'Thanks,' said Katie, thinking she was going to need more than luck to keep Edward happy for the next few days.

Edward wasn't in his room. That surprised Katie. She'd been sure that he'd either be watching television or on his Playstation. She hovered outside his door, wondering where to look for him next.

Poppy opened her eyes. Yawning lazily, she stretched out her legs. She'd had a wonderful cat nap lying in a pool of sunlight, and now she was full of energy and ready to play. She looked around to see what the other kittens

were doing. Suki was sitting by the window, washing her white tummy. On silent paws, Poppy crept up and jumped on her. Hissing with surprise, Suki spun round. Poppy gave her a playful cuff. Suki leapt at Poppy and cuffed her back, then ran away.

Chase!

Poppy hared after Suki and soon the two kittens were tearing around the room, hiding and leaping

out at each other. Poppy dived through the
cat tunnel. Suki came after her and Poppy
lay in wait, pouncing on Suki as she came
out the other end. Suki twisted free and
somehow landed on top of Poppy. Playfully
they rolled together on the ground until the
boot room door opened.

Glancing up, Poppy tensed. It was that boy
again. She pushed Suki off and sat up
warily with her tail
wrapped around her
paws. What did he
want this time?
Poppy couldn't work
him out. Sometimes
she thought he was
trying to make
friends and

sometimes he was very unkind. Like earlier this morning. He'd given her a cat treat and as she was eating it, he'd started to tie a bell to her tail. Poppy's tail twitched at the memory. She hadn't liked that — tails weren't meant to have things tied to them. She'd struggled like mad, then Katie arrived and Edward was suddenly nice again.

So what did he want this time?

Poppy stared at him mistrustfully.

'Here, puss.' Crouching down, Edward rubbed his thumb against his fingers.

Poppy hesitated but she didn't hold out for long. She knew that action meant she was going to be stroked or if she was very lucky she'd get a cuddle. She stretched out her neck. Edward continued calling her. He was smiling and his voice was soft and friendly. Cautiously, Poppy stepped closer and Edward slowly pulled his other hand from behind his back. What had he got there? Poppy moved closer, hoping for a cat treat. Suddenly, a jet of cold water hit her in the chest.

Whiskers!

Squeaking in surprise, Poppy jumped back. Where had that come from?

Edward was clutching his stomach and

making a horrible sound. Poppy stared at him. Was he hurt? Another blast of water hit her neck. Edward rolled on the floor, still making the awful noise.

He was laughing! Poppy was very put out. Why was the boy laughing? What was funny about getting wet? Poppy fluffed out her soggy coat, hoping to make herself look bigger. Arching her back, she hissed indignantly. Edward seemed to find that even funnier. He sat up and pointed something at her. Then he squeezed his fingers and a blast of water soaked Poppy again.

'Meow!'

She fled in the opposite direction, but there was no escape from Edward and his icy stream of water. Even when Poppy hid inside the cat tunnel, Edward ran round and shot water at her from the other end. It made the floor slippery and hard to stand up. Poppy almost fell over trying to get out again. She stared around looking for somewhere else to hide. Maybe if she got behind that very tall pair of boots? Shaking with fright, Poppy dived towards them.

When Princess Katie opened the boot room door she gasped with shock. What did Edward think he was doing, chasing after Poppy with that enormous water pistol? Red spots of anger danced before Katie's eyes.

'Edward! Stop it right now!' Edward was having so much fun that he didn't see Katie come in or hear her shout. He ran after Poppy, backing her into a corner behind a tall pair of riding boots.

'Stop!' roared Katie, going after him and grabbing his arm.

'Get off!' said Edward, shaking her away. His eyes were wide with excitement and he could hardly stand for laughing. He fired the water pistol again as Katie knocked his arm upwards. A jet of water shot out, missing Poppy and hitting the wall.

'Get off me!'

Impatiently, Edward shook Katie free and fired again. The water pistol spluttered. A few drops of water spurted from the end. Edward kept pumping but there was only a dribble of water left.

'Empty!' he said in disgust, throwing it on the floor.

At once Katie snatched it up. 'How dare you!' she yelled.

Edward stared at her in surprise. 'It was only a bit of fun.'

'Fun!' shouted Katie. 'Look at Poppy. Can't you see she's terrified?'

'Whatever is going on?'

Katie had been going to pick Poppy up but, hearing the queen's carefully controlled voice, she spun round.

'Mum!'

The queen raised up a questioning eyebrow.

Stepping forward, Edward spoke in an apologetic voice. 'I'm sorry about the mess, Auntie. I suppose this is my fault. Katie wanted a go with my new water pistol.'

'I see,' said the queen. Glaring at Katie, she said in a low voice, 'I'm very disappointed in you. Surely you're old enough to know that

a water pistol is an outdoor toy. Look at this mess!'

'But —' said Katie.

'Please don't interrupt. I don't mind you playing with water but not inside the palace. And I never want to hear you shouting like that again. Princesses do not shout. And they do not wear jodhpurs indoors. When you've cleared up this mess, then you will change into something more suitable. Edward, take your new toy into the garden, please. Katie will join you shortly.'

'Yes, Auntie,' said Edward, meekly.

Sending Katie a triumphant look over his shoulder, he scurried after the queen.

Katie clenched her fists. It was bad enough

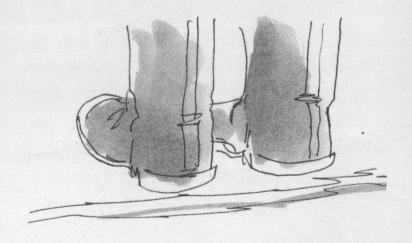

getting the blame for Edward's mess but she was even more worried about his behaviour. She had to stop him from teasing Poppy. He thought it was funny, but it wasn't. Teasing Poppy was *cruel*.

Poppy was cowering in the corner behind the boots. Her sodden fur stuck out in spiky clumps and her ears were back. She gazed up at Katie with sad green eyes. Swallowing

back tears, Katie picked her up and cradled her in her arms.

'It's OK. You're safe now,' she said, as she gently dried Poppy's matted fur on her T-shirt.

Chapter 7

Escape

Edward didn't want to play with Katie any more. He spent the rest of the day in his room, glued to his Playstation. Katie didn't mind. At least she didn't have to worry that he might be teasing her kittens. She spent a fun afternoon with Becky, rolling balls for the kittens to chase.

The following morning at breakfast, the queen had exciting news. 'Grandma and Grandad are coming for lunch today.'

Katie and Edward shared one set of grandparents and Edward brightened immediately.

'Hooray,' he cheered. 'I haven't seen them for ages.'

'Lunch will be at one o' clock,' said the queen. 'So make sure you're here on time. What are you doing today?'

'Playstation,' said Edward before Katie could answer.

'Oh no, darling,' said Auntie Meg. 'You play that all the time at home. I'm sure Katie's arranged something wonderful for you to do together.'

'Swimming,' said Katie, glancing at Edward.

'It's too cold,' said Edward with a shiver.

'In the indoor pool,' Katie added.

Edward said nothing.

'The lifeguard said he'd get the inflatables out. I've got a new one. It's great fun. It's got a slide and a water cannon.'

'I've got lots of inflatables at home,' said Edward in a bored voice. 'My favourite is the castle with a proper drawbridge and a water-squirting dragon.'

Katie smiled politely as Edward carried on boasting. But even though he claimed that his swimming pool and inflatable toys were much bigger and better than Katie's, he seemed to enjoy himself in Starlight Palace's pool. His favourite game was squirting Katie and Becky with the water cannon. Katie didn't mind. It was fun being splashed and she'd rather Edward was

shooting water at her than Poppy.

After swimming, Katie was secretly relieved when Edward refused her invitation to go and play in the gardens, saying he was going to his room.

'Let's take the kittens outside with us,' Becky suggested. 'Poppy loved going out.'

Katie hesitated. She wasn't keen on the idea but knew she couldn't keep the kittens shut indoors forever.

'We won't go far. We'll stay in the bit of garden that's fenced,' said Becky.

'OK,' said Katie at last. 'Just for a short time.'

The boot room had a door that led straight to the gardens. A small area was fenced to make it more private for the royal family. Propping open the door, Katie and Becky went outside. A few minutes later, Pixie stuck his nose out.

He sniffed the air before boldly crossing the patio.

Becky nudged Katie. 'Look,' she whispered.

'Pixie's used to the outdoors.' Katie smiled, remembering how, when she'd first got the kittens, Pixie had wandered off and nearly spent a night in the woods on his own.

Bella was quick to follow and, shortly after, Poppy cautiously stuck her  head out and looked around.

'Prrrip!' she squeaked, jumping into the garden with an excited flick of her tail.

The other kittens took a little longer to brave the big outdoors, but soon, six little cats were exploring the garden. As they grew bolder, they went a little further, sniffing under bushes and chasing butterflies. Katie

didn't take her eyes off them, but gradually
she began to relax. The kittens were having
so much fun, what was there to worry
about? A while later, Mrs Philips came to
the boot room door with a jug of squash
and a plate of cookies.

'How did your mum guess I was starving
hungry?' Katie asked, getting up to collect
the tray.

'She knew we were swimming and we're
always starving afterwards,' Becky chuckled.

As Katie took the tray, Becky said, 'There
aren't any glasses. Shall I run in and get
them?'

'Silly me! Thanks, darling, that would be a
big help,' said Mrs Philips.

Becky ran off while Katie put the tray on
the patio table.

'Where's Prince Edward?' asked Mrs Philips. 'I'll go and tell him there's a drink and cookies here or he won't last until lunchtime.' 'I'll go,' said Katie. Edward was her responsibility. She glanced at the kittens playing together on the lawn. They seemed happy enough. It wouldn't take long to run up to Edward's room.

Taking a deep breath, she slowly huffed it back out to get rid of the wobbly nervous feeling that leaving the kittens alone gave her. She was being silly. The kittens would be fine while she was gone. Katie quickly ran indoors. She reached Edward's room in one minute flat but there was no answer.

'Edward?' Katie opened the door and peered inside.

The room was empty.

By the time Katie got back to the garden, Becky was pouring squash into three glasses.

'Have you seen Edward?' she asked, breathlessly.

Becky shook her head as she handed her a drink.

Katie sighed. 'I'd better go and find him.'

'I'll come with you.'

'Thanks, but I might be a while. You stay here with the kittens. They're having so much fun. If you come too then . . .' Katie broke off suddenly. Her heart thumped loudly as she scanned the garden, counting the kittens.

One, two, three, four, five . . .

Katie's eyes darted everywhere, but there were definitely only five cats playing on the lawn. So who was missing?

'Where's Poppy?' she asked, her voice rising in alarm.

Becky looked around. Calmly she said, 'She won't have gone far. She's probably hiding.'

'Poppy!'

Loudly calling her name, Katie and Becky hunted in the bushes and flower beds. They searched everywhere twice, but Poppy had totally disappeared.

Katie was trying her best to stay calm when a horrible thought set her heart thundering.

'Becky,' she said slowly, 'do you think it's a coincidence that Edward and Poppy are both missing?'

Poppy loved being outdoors. The air was full of exciting smells and the sun on her

whiskers felt wonderful. She pranced around chasing a butterfly until she lost it and found herself in the bushes. Poppy's tail twitched with excitement. The smells here were different – they reminded her of the place with the tall hedges. She'd liked it there. It was mysterious and full of interesting noises. Suddenly, Poppy longed to be there again.

And for once there was nothing stopping her.

Excitedly, she kept on going, weaving her way through the shrubs and plants until she came to a fence.

'Prrrip!' said Poppy crossly. Now she was very curious to see what was on the other side.

She followed the fence a little way until she came to a gate. Poppy couldn't believe her luck. There was a small gap under it. Dropping to the ground she made herself as flat as possible as she wriggled through to the other side. That was easy! But which way should she go now? Poppy looked left and right. One way was blocked by a large bird with a bright blue head and a long neck. Poppy loved birds, but this one was

much bigger than her, so she set off in the opposite direction.

A little while later, she caught a familiar scent. Standing still, she delicately sniffed the air. That set her whiskers twitching! Recognising the smell, Poppy hurried on until she reached a tall, green hedge. She trotted alongside it, past the bench and on to an opening. She'd found it! The way in! Tail aloft, Poppy entered the maze.

Chapter 8

Poppy Makes a Friend

The maze was every bit as good as Poppy remembered. She wandered along, enjoying the feeling of being in a tunnel as she made her way between the tall hedges. This time, there was no one to hurry her up. When she heard an interesting rustle or a squeak, Poppy stopped to investigate. Mostly, she saw tails or feathers disappearing into the branches, but once she was lucky and came face to face with a mouse. For a second, Poppy and the mouse stared at each other. Then, as she reached out to give it a friendly cuff, the mouse dived and was swallowed up by the green leaves.

Sometimes Poppy discovered a hedge blocking the path. Then she'd turn around and try another way. It was such fun. Her brothers and sisters would love it. She should go and get them! Poppy was about to turn back when she heard a funny noise. She stood still, one paw raised in the air, her ears pricked forward. There it was again! Whatever was making such a strange sound?

Poppy didn't like it. Cautiously, she turned away until after a bit she couldn't go any further. A wall of green was stopping her. The noise was coming closer. Poppy stood tall, fluffing out her fur to make her body look bigger. Then her ears flattened with fear as Edward blundered round the corner.

'Coincidence,' panted Becky as she ran through the palace gardens.

Katie crossed her fingers and hoped that

Becky was right. But what if it wasn't a coincidence? What if Edward had taken Poppy away? Surely he wouldn't do anything mean? But the trouble with Edward was that he didn't seem to realise that teasing an animal was cruel.

'It's almost lunchtime,' said Katie, checking her watch. 'I'm going to be late, but I can't go back without Poppy and Edward.'

'There's one place we haven't looked yet,' said Becky, pulling up.

Katie stopped and stared at Becky. 'Not the maze!' she said.

'It's the only place left,' said Becky.

'Why would Edward take Poppy to the maze?'

'I don't know,' said Becky, quietly.

Katie's mind raced with possibilities. Had Edward left Poppy in the maze to see if she could find her way home? Nothing would surprise her, but panicking about it wasn't going to help. The best thing she could do now was to check the maze. She set off again with Becky running at her side.

Poppy stared at the hedge, wondering if she

could climb up it to escape. Then she realised Edward was standing very still and, strangely, he had water leaking from his eyes. Furiously he wiped it away with the back of his hand.

'I'm lost,' he said. 'I wanted to play on the fort but I couldn't find the middle. Now I can't get out. I've been trying for ages, but I keep going round in circles. I'm going to be stuck here for hours and I'll miss lunch with Grandma and Grandad. I might even miss tea. If no one finds me then I could be here all night!'

Poppy stared at him. Was he being friendly or was this another trick? She didn't fancy having things tied to her tail or water squirted at her again. She took a slow step backwards and ended up with her bottom squashed against the hedge. Spinning round, she tried to wriggle under it.

'Wait!' Edward sounded frightened. 'I've been going round in circles for ages. Don't leave me.'

This part of the hedge was too thick to climb through. Reluctantly, Poppy turned back. Edward sat down, reached out and, rubbing his fingers together, called Poppy to him.

Poppy stared back scornfully. Did he really think she was that stupid? He'd caught her out like that too many times before. She wondered if she should make a run for it. If she was quick, she might be able to get past Edward, but, as she bunched her body, ready to spring, Edward let out a loud sob.

'I'm scared.'

The drops of water ran down his face and splashed on the ground. Disdainfully, Poppy shook a paw. Yuk! Edward wasn't squirting the water at her deliberately though and she sensed his fear and unhappiness. Suddenly, she felt sorry for him. She crept closer and nudged him with her nose.

Edward looked as shocked as she felt. Why had she done that? What if this was another trick? But somehow she knew it wasn't. As Edward reached forward, Poppy stood very still and was rewarded with a stroke on the top of her head.

'I'm sorry I was mean to you. You're going think I'm a baby and so would Katie – that's why I never told her and tried to act grown up. The thing is, I'm scared of cats. I got badly scratched by one when I was little, near my eye – I could have gone blind. But you're not really a scratchy cat, are you?'

Poppy didn't have a clue what Edward was saying, but he seemed friendlier. Nudging his hand, she slipped round him and walked away.

'Follow me,' she purred.

When Edward didn't move, Poppy turned back and nudged his hand again. She had to nudge him several more times before he finally got it.

'Oh! You want me to follow you. Really? Do you know the way back then?'

'Meow!' said Poppy impatiently. Was he coming or not?

'You do, don't you?' Edward gave a shaky laugh. 'And I thought cats were stupid. I've been wrong about lots of things, haven't I? Come on, then, show me where to go.'

Just as Katie and Becky were about to enter the maze, they saw Edward following Poppy out of it.

'Poppy!' Katie pounced and protectively swept the kitten up. 'Are you all right?'

Hugging Poppy to her, she glared at

Edward. 'What's going on?'

'I got lost,' said Edward, quietly. 'Poppy found me and showed me the way out.'

Katie stared back in disbelief.

'I know what you're thinking and I'm sorry. I was scared of your cats at first. All those things I did to Poppy – I thought I was being brave and funny, but I wasn't. Poppy's a cool kitten and I think she's forgiven me.'

'Well, if Poppy's forgiven you, then I should too,' said Katie.

'Thanks,' said Edward, shyly.

A loud gong made everyone jump.

'Lunchtime,' said Katie. 'We'd better hurry or we'll be late for Grandma and Grandad.'

'I'll take Poppy back,' offered Becky generously. 'See you later everyone!'

Lunch was fun and Edward seemed to be enjoying it too, but Katie couldn't help feeling a little suspicious when he disappeared the moment it was over. Her suspicions grew

when she went to look for him, but he wasn't in his bedroom. Where had he gone? Katie went straight to the boot room. She could hear someone giggling. Catching her breath, she went in.

'Edward!'

Guiltily he looked up. Poppy was eating a king prawn that he'd smuggled out from lunch. Then she curled up on his lap as he stroked her gently.

'I . . . I came to say thank you to Poppy,' he stammered. 'You won't tell, will you?'

Katie started to laugh. 'About the prawns, or about you giving Poppy a cuddle?'

'The prawns,' said Edward, chuckling too. 'Poppy's great. I like her and I don't mind who knows it.'

'Good,' said Princess Katie, 'because Poppy definitely likes you too.'

Win a kitten charm bracelet!

To enter this competition, help Princess Katie
unscramble the name of Poppy's favourite toy:

☆ **M S U O E** ☆

We will put all the correct entries into a draw
and select one lucky winner!
Go online to send us your answer at

PrincessKatiesKittens.co.uk

or send your entry on a postcard to:
Princess Katie's Kittens Competition,
Piccadilly Press, 5 Castle Road, London, NW1 8PR.
Don't forget to include your name and address.

☆ Good luck! ☆

Competition closes 26th October 2012.

Competition only open to UK and Republic of Ireland residents.
No purchase necessary. For full terms and conditions please see
www.princesskatieskittens.co.uk.

☆ Meet a new cute kitten in every adventure! ☆

Pixie
at the Palace

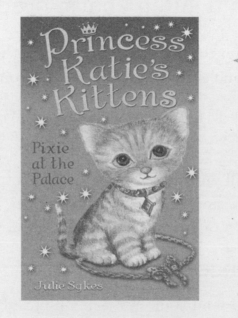

One of the newly found kittens has gone missing in the woods. Can Princess Katie and her best friend Becky find Pixie and bring him safely back to Starlight Palace?

Bella
at the Ball

Princess Katie is busy preparing for the queen's magnificent birthday ball, but Bella is busy getting into mischief! Katie and Becky must hurry to put things right, or the whole ball will be ruined!

★ Coming soon ★

Suki in the Snow

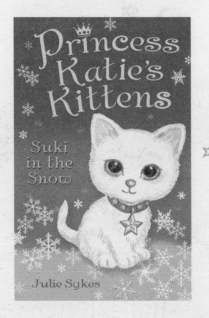

Suki has crept into Princess Katie's luggage and has come on her skiing holiday!
But when Suki tries to make her own way home, Katie and Becky race against time to find the kitten lost in the snow.

Princess Katie's Kittens

PrincessKatiesKittens.co.uk

Secret facts about the kittens
Kitten puzzles and activities
Princess Katie's top kitten care tips
Competitions
Book news and more!